A Love to Remember: A Tale of Redemption and True Love

Harper Knight

Published by RWG Publishing, 2023.

This is a work of fiction. Similarities to real people, places, or events are entirely coincidental.

A LOVE TO REMEMBER: A TALE OF REDEMPTION AND TRUE LOVE

First edition. March 30, 2023.

Copyright © 2023 Harper Knight.

Written by Harper Knight.

Also by Harper Knight

The Last Dance: A Love Affair with Destiny
A Love to Remember: A Tale of Redemption and True Love

Table of Contents

Note From the Editor 1
Chapter 1: The One That Got Away 3
Chapter 2: A Chance Encounter 5
Chapter 3: Learning to Forgive 9
Chapter 4: The Sweetest Kind of Romance 11
Chapter 5: A Leap of Faith 13
Chapter 6: Confronting the Past 15
Chapter 7: Overcoming Fear 19
Chapter 8: Falling in Love All Over Again 21
Chapter 9: A Promise to Keep 23
Chapter 10: The First Date 25
Chapter 11: A Surprising Turn of Events 27
Chapter 12: A Heartfelt Confession 29
Chapter 13: A Complicated Family Dynamic 31
Chapter 14: A Romantic Getaway 33
Chapter 15: A Bump in the Road 35
Chapter 16: Uncovering the Truth 37
Chapter 17: A Moment of Doubt 39
Chapter 18: Holding On to Hope 41
Chapter 19: A Life-Changing Decision 43
Chapter 20: A Love Tested 45
Chapter 21: The Power of Forgiveness 47
Chapter 22: Building a Future Together 49
Chapter 23: A Celebration of Love 51
Chapter 24: The Wedding Day 53
Chapter 25: Happily Ever After 55
Chapter 26: Memories to Last a Lifetime 57

Note From the Editor

This book is not written in real time. It has memory backflashes to prepare you for the next chapters. I enjoyed it and I hope you do to.

   Grace Vincent

Chapter 1: The One That Got Away

Emma stood by the window, staring out at the street below. It was a beautiful day, but she couldn't bring herself to enjoy it. Her mind kept wandering back to the past - to a time when she had been young and foolish and let the love of her life slip away.

She had been in college then, and had met Jack in one of her classes. They had hit it off immediately, and had started dating soon after. Emma had never been so happy - Jack was everything she could have wanted in a partner. But then life got in the way. Jack's father had died suddenly, and he had to drop out of college to help support his family. Emma had wanted to stay with him, to help him through this difficult time, but Jack had pushed her away. He didn't want her to give up her own dreams for him.

Emma had been heartbroken when Jack broke up with her. She had tried to move on, but no one ever measured up to Jack. Eventually, she had given up and focused on her career instead. She had become a successful journalist, but the ache in her heart remained.

Now, years later, Emma was back in town for her high school reunion. She had sworn to herself that she wouldn't let Jack get to her, that she would be cool and collected and show him that she had moved on. But as she looked out at the street, she knew that she had been lying to herself. She still loved him, and she always would.

As she turned away from the window, the phone rang. It was her best friend, Lucy, who was also in town for the reunion. "Hey, Em," Lucy said. "I'm outside your hotel. Let's grab lunch before the reunion tonight."

Emma agreed, grateful for the distraction. She met Lucy outside, and they walked to a nearby café. As they sat down, Lucy leaned in. "So, have you seen him yet?"

Emma knew exactly who Lucy was talking about. "No," she said, trying to sound nonchalant. "I'm not sure I want to."

Lucy rolled her eyes. "Come on, Emma. It's been years. You need closure. And who knows, maybe he's still single and available."

Emma shook her head. "I don't want to get my hopes up. Besides, we were young then. It's not like we're the same people now."

Lucy smiled. "You won't know unless you try. And I heard he's been asking around about you."

Emma's heart skipped a beat. "What? Who told you that?"

Lucy shrugged. "Just a little birdie. Look, Emma, you don't have to do anything you don't want to. But I think you should at least talk to him tonight. You never know what might happen."

Emma thought about it for a moment. She knew Lucy was right - she needed closure. And if Jack really was still interested in her, then maybe they could give it another shot. It was a long shot, but it was better than always wondering what could have been.

"Okay," Emma said, finally. "I'll talk to him tonight. But I'm not getting my hopes up."

Lucy grinned. "That's the spirit."

As they finished their lunch, Emma couldn't help but feel a sense of excitement. Maybe this reunion would turn out to be more than just a chance to catch up with old classmates. Maybe it would be the start of something new - or the rekindling of something old and special.

Emma just had to wait and see.

Chapter 2: A Chance Encounter

When Emma finally made it to the reunion, it was in full swing. Balloons and streamers adorned the gymnasium, while a DJ played hits from the '90s. Emma recognized a few of her old classmates and greeted them warmly. She kept looking for Jack, but she couldn't find him.

Emma's disappointment grew as the evening progressed. Perhaps Lucy was mistaken in assuming that Jack wanted to see her again. Perhaps he was fully over it.

When she turned around to go, she saw him across the room. Although he had clearly aged, his good looks had not diminished. When she approached him, she had a sudden surge of nervousness.

Hey, she tapped him on the shoulder and said.

When he did, they stood there gaping at each other. After that, his grin made Emma feel twenty years younger.

Emma, he greeted her. "Nice to see you again."

"It's lovely to see you too," was her reply. To ask, "How are you doing?"

They spent some time chatting and reminiscing. Jack informed her that his mom and sister were doing fine, but that his brother had hit hard times. Emma informed him of her occupation, her travels, and her overall status in life.

Emma felt a wave of nostalgia rush over her as they talked. It was as if no time had passed at all between them. How natural it was to chat with Jack and how much they shared in common had slipped her mind.

Jack took a break to go fetch some beverages for everyone. As she saw him leave, Emma had a pang of regret. If he had only let her stay with him when his father died, they might have been able to make things work. Perhaps a life together would have been possible for them.

Someone patted her on the shoulder as she was deep in concentration. Lucy, who appeared to be rather ecstatic.

Lucy smiled and remarked to Emma, "Emma, you won't believe who just walked in."

Emma's eyebrows went up. "Who?"

Lucy pointed out the door and said, "Your old flame."

Emma's stomach dropped. By the time Jack returned with the drinks, he had overheard everything that had been spoken.

Emma got up and said, "Excuse me." "I have some business to attend to."

She made her way over to Lucy, her face red with shame. She yelled at him, "Why did you have to say it in front of him?"

Lucy appeared perplexed. I'm confused by what you're saying.

Emma's eyes rolled. You referred to Jack as "your old flame," so you understand what I mean.

Lucy seemed repentant. Sorry, Em, I didn't want to offend you; I just knew you were looking forward to seeing him.

Emma let out a long sigh. It's true, but I don't want him to believe I'm still obsessed with him, so I won't let on.

Lucy acknowledged this with a nod. "Listen, I get it. Look, put it out of your mind.

She inhaled deeply and then slowly exhaled. "OK, thanks, Lucy. I appreciate it."

It was a happy grin that Lucy wore. Friends are there for times like that, so of course.

When Emma redirected her attention back to Jack, he was already out of sight. She looked around the room, but she couldn't find him. A twinge of disappointment stabbed at her. Perhaps she'd blown it. Perhaps this was her one and only chance meeting, and she blew it.

But then she spotted him again, this time standing at the gym's window. With some trepidation, she made her way closer to him.

Hello, she called out.

He merely mumbled, "Hello," before returning his gaze to the window.

"I apologize for earlier," Emma said. My friend wasn't trying to hurt my feelings, and I'm over being obsessed with you.

When he faced her, Jack's eyes flashed with emotion, and Emma caught a glimpse of it. He smiled slightly and replied, "I'm not sure I believe you."

Emma's heart sped up a bit. I mean, "why not?"

"Because I'm not fully over you either," he added, his eyes never leaving hers.

Emma felt confused and disoriented. Was he really saying what she took him to mean? Did he still feel the same way about her?

Jack grabbed her hand before she could utter a word. As I think about you, Emma, I often wonder if we made the correct choice back then. I'll never know what may have been.

Emma felt her eyes well up with tears. "Jack, I-"

But as Jack leant in for a kiss, she couldn't finish. All the tension and animosity that had built up between them over the years exploded like rockets.

Once they backed off, Emma felt weightless. She finally squeaked out, "Jack," after a long pause. I'd never have guessed-"

Nevertheless, her thought was cut off mid-sentence. She had allowed herself to be drawn in for another kiss from Jack.

While they were kissing, Emma felt like the puzzle pieces of her life were coming together. She was determined to make the most of her second chance with her soul mate. No matter what happened, she vowed to herself that she would never let Jack go again.

Chapter 3: Learning to Forgive

Emma felt happy and fulfilled when she awoke the following morning. She'd spent the night with Jack, and they'd spent the time talking and joking and making up for lost time. They had touched lightly, kissed and hugged, but not gone any farther. Simply being in one other's company had been gratifying.

Emma was about to go to sleep when she remembered they still had a lot to discuss. They both had baggage from previous relationships that needed to be resolved if they were going to make this one work.

She hurriedly got ready and left for breakfast at the hotel's restaurant. Jack was there waiting for her, and he appeared anxious.

"Hello," she greeted him as she sat down opposite him.

He replied, "Hello," as he continued to nibble on his cereal. To begin, "Last night..."

Emma anticipated his next words. She inhaled deeply. Can we just be together, Jack, without thinking about everything else? I know we have a lot to talk about, but for now, can we just enjoy this moment?

Jack turned his warm gaze toward her. He reached across the table and took her hand, saying, "Alright." "Okay."

They got together and spent the day walking around town and talking about the good old days. They reconnected, chatted about old times, and laughed and joked like old times. As if no time had passed at all, they reunited.

Emma had something important to say as they strolled along the shore. "Jack, I have to say I'm sorry."

Jack gave her a perplexed glance. To what end?"

"For not being there for you when your dad died," Emma replied, her voice shaking. I'm sorry I left you and abandoned you; I should have stuck by you.

There was a visible change in Jack's expression. I didn't want you to sacrifice your goals for mine, so please don't feel obligated to say you're sorry, Emma.

To this, Emma shook her head. That's no reason why I wasn't there for you, though; you needed me no matter what.

Jack picked her up and cradled her in his strong arms. I forgive you, Emma; I get why you took the decisions you did; and I'm not without fault either; I should have gone out to you, even when I was struggling.

Emma felt her eyes well up with tears. "Jack, I've always loved you, and I want you to know that."

Jack planted a kiss on her head. I love you too, Emma, and I believe we can make it work if we can find it in ourselves to forgive one other and the past.

Emma nodded, finally feeling at ease. The past was already set, and Jack was correct. But, they are capable of working together toward a bright future that is full of love and forgiveness.

Emma felt a sense of coming home as they strolled along the beach hand in hand. She finally returned home to Jack, to herself, and to the love that had been waiting for her the whole time.

Chapter 4: The Sweetest Kind of Romance

Emma and Jack spent the next few days exploring the town and enjoying each other's company. They went to the beach, visited old haunts, and tried new restaurants. It was like they were on a second honeymoon.

As they walked along the pier one afternoon, Emma felt a sense of contentment wash over her. This was what she had always wanted - a partner who loved and supported her, who shared her values and passions. Jack was all of those things and more.

They stopped at a small ice cream shop, and Jack bought them each a cone. They sat on a bench, licking their ice cream and people-watching.

"This is the sweetest kind of romance," Emma said, smiling at Jack.

Jack grinned. "What, ice cream on a bench?"

Emma laughed. "No, silly. Being with someone who makes you happy, who makes every moment feel special."

Jack took her hand. "That's how I feel when I'm with you. Like everything is a little bit brighter, a little bit sweeter."

Emma leaned her head on his shoulder, feeling overwhelmed with emotion. "Jack, I never thought I could be this happy."

Jack wrapped his arm around her. "You deserve to be happy, Emma. You always have. And I'm going to do everything I can to make sure you stay that way."

Emma looked up at him, feeling a rush of love. She had always known that Jack was special, but she had forgotten just how special. He was the missing piece in her life, the one she had been searching for all along.

As they finished their ice cream and walked back to the hotel, Emma felt like she was walking on clouds. She knew that there would be challenges ahead - old wounds to heal, new obstacles to overcome - but she also knew that they could face them together.

She was finally living the sweetest kind of romance, and she wasn't going to let anything get in the way of that.

Chapter 5: A Leap of Faith

Emma and Jack knew they had to make a choice as the end of the week drew near. Back in the city, Emma had a job, friends, and a regular routine. Jack was a family man with a lot on his plate. They couldn't remain in this perfect community indefinitely.

They both hated the idea of being separated from one another. They were in love again and didn't want to lose each other.

Emma broke her silence as they watched the sunset from the hotel balcony. I don't want to be without you, Jack. I don't want to go back to the way things were.

Jack turned his warm gaze toward her. Like you, Emma, I don't want to be separated from you, but we can't afford to be reckless.

Emma acknowledged this with a nod. I understand, but what if there wasn't? What if we could find a way to be together without giving up everything else?

Jack's interest was peaked as he studied her. As in, "What do you mean?"

Emma inhaled deeply. Is it possible that we could live together?

Jack's pupils drew in. That's a huge accomplishment, Emma.

It's true," Emma admitted. But we've worked together before, we trust each other, and we have a long history together.

Jack gave a tentative nod. It's just that I'm afraid of the consequences if things don't go as planned.

Emma reached for his hand. I love you, Jack, so much that I'm willing to take a chance and find out if this works.

Jack gave her a serious look as he glanced at her. This isn't something we can just erase, so I want to be sure you're sure, Emma.

Emma acknowledged this with a nod. "I want to take a chance on us," she said. "I don't want to spend the rest of my life wondering what may have been."

Jack inhaled deeply. "Alright, OK, let's get to it."

Emma felt a mixture of excitement and nervousness as they packed up their belongings and checked out of the motel. This was an enormous move, but it was the right one.

They located a modest city apartment not far from Emma's workplace. They moved in together and took many weeks to unpack, decorate, and settle in. Problems arose, to be sure, such as arguments about who should do what or who should have more room, but they were resolved with love and patience.

Emma knew she had made the right choice as they fell into their new routine. Together, she and Jack were creating a life they both enjoyed. They had gambled on an uncertain outcome, but it had paid off.

One night, while snuggling on the couch, Emma turned to Jack. She finally managed to get out a thank you. Thank you "for having faith in me."

Jack cracked a grin. "I love you, Emma. Thank you for giving me a chance."

Emma felt her eyes well up with tears. You have my undying affection as well, Jack.

As they kissed, Emma realized that theirs was the purest form of love: one based on mutual faith, forgiveness, and trust. And she appreciated it every single day.

Chapter 6: Confronting the Past

During the course of several months, Emma and Jack developed a pleasant routine. During the weekends, they would hang out, cook, and watch movies together. Emma felt like she was in a dream, and it was a dream she didn't want to end.

Yet, she did have one niggling concern. She never dealt with the trauma that had caused her to run away from her hometown and from Jack. She understood that confronting it was the only way to finally go on.

She planned a trip back to the origin of her troubles. Jack accompanied her on this journey and was there for her the whole time.

As driving through the neighborhood, Emma began to feel uneasy. As she had avoided this area for so long, it was as if she were experiencing it for the first time.

They went to a cafe where Emma had worked during her time at university. Marie, the proprietor, was very friendly and welcoming.

Marie embraced Emma and remarked, "Emma, it's so lovely to see you." Someone asked, "Who is this dashing young man?"

Emma felt a surge of satisfaction as she presented Jack to the group. She was determined to broadcast the news that she had finally achieved peace of mind and was ready to put the past in the past.

Marie inquired into Emma's personal life as they were sipping coffee together. Emma paused, uncertain of how much information to give.

And then, "I'm doing well," she said at last. "I'm in a relationship with the love of my life and doing work that fulfills me."

With a grin, Marie greeted the world. That's great news, honey; you merit every bit of success in life.

Emma felt her eyes well up with tears. Marie had been like a second mother to her for as long as she could remember, thus Marie's encouragement meant more than words can express.

Emma felt as though she were reliving a fond memory as they strolled through the streets of the town. She showed him around the park, the movie theater, and the diner where they used to have pancakes at 2 in the morning.

They reached Emma's childhood residence at last. It appeared smaller than she recalled, but just as dilapidated. As she reached the door, a wave of melancholy overcame her.

Jack grasped her hand and squeezed it comfortingly. Can you handle this?

Emma acknowledged this with a nod. "I need to be."

Emma's heart was racing when they knocked on the door. She had no idea what was going to happen. Both of her parents were long dead and absent when she was little. Could you expect anyone to be there?

A middle-aged woman with bleary eyes walked through the open door. "May I be of service?"

After a little pause, Emma spoke out. "Hello, my name is Emma and I'm simply visiting because I used to reside in this area many years ago."

After a brief exchange of gazes, the woman nodded. To enter, say.

Emma experienced déjà vu as they entered. Although the furniture had changed, the room's basic layout remained unchanged. She had flashbacks to her younger self, chasing herself down the halls and ducking into her bedroom.

Karen, the current owner of the residence, is who the woman presented herself as. She detailed the fixes and alterations she had done for them. Emma listened courteously, but she wasn't really paying attention.

She worked up the nerve to inquire at last. "Karen, did my father leave any hints as to what happened to him?"

Karen gazed at her with a compassionate expression. The house was abandoned when I acquired it, and it took a lot of work, but I'm sorry, Emma; I can't tell you anything about your father.

Emma was overcome by a wave of disappointment. She was searching for resolution, for reasons. But, she realized that was unrealistic.

Emma sported a phony grin and added, "I understand." "We appreciate you showing us around the house."

Karen indicated with a nod that she wished to continue. Before she could finish, though, Jack chimed in.

He took Emma's hand and thanked her for her time. "Let's go ahead and leave."

Emma felt lonely as they walked away from the home and toward the car. She was looking forward to finally putting her past behind her. But, her search had yielded no results.

Jack felt her dissatisfaction. How are you feeling?

To this, Emma shook her head. I don't know, I guess I was just expecting more.

Jack put an arm around her. "Emma, you're constructing a new life now, with me. That's all that matters. You don't need closure from your past."

Emma turned her eyes to him, her heart filled with appreciation. The guy was right. She was fine without knowing what happened before. She was going into the future with someone who cared about her and would always have her back.

Emma felt at calm as they drove back to their flat. After facing her past, she gained some insight but not the answers she was seeking.

She was prepared to go on to better things in the future. In addition, she realized that with Jack by her side, she could accomplish anything.

Chapter 7: Overcoming Fear

Emma was naturally wary about new situations. She was quite cautious and preferred to always play it safe. Yet, she had learned from her time with Jack that there are times when you just have to take a chance.

Jack arrived home from work giddy one night. He said, "Guess what?" with a gleam in his eye.

Intrigued, Emma asked, "What?"

I've always wanted to attend to the hot air balloon festival that's happening this weekend, but I've never had somebody to go with.

Fear began to rise in Emma's stomach. Gas-filled balloons? That sounded extremely risky. Yet she dreaded breaking Jack's heart.

She attempted enthusiasm and responded, "Yes, that sounds fun."

Jack beamed a broad grin. In that case, I'll get us tickets.

Emma began to feel anxious as the weekend neared. She felt uncomfortable at the prospect of flying through the air in a hot air balloon because she had never been in one before.

Yet she couldn't go back on her word now. She didn't want to disappoint Jack, who was quite eager to get started.

Emma's heart was racing as they approached the festival grounds. All around them, balloons of every size and color towered over the onlookers. The warmth of the burners reached her face.

Jack grasped her hand and squeezed it comfortingly. "Emma, don't worry; this is fantastic."

They joined a random assortment of people in the balloon's basket. As the balloon steadily rose, Emma's stomach began to feel like it was about to fall out from under her.

Yet, as they continued to climb, she began to feel a rush of excitement. They were able to see for miles in every direction, and the landscape spread out below them like a colorful quilt.

Jack named the various landmarks he and Emma passed along the way. She felt as though she suddenly had new perspectives on life.

When they touched down again, Emma felt a sense of satisfaction. She had overcome her apprehension, and the result had been fantastic.

Jack gave her an intense embrace. I told you it would be fantastic, and here it is!

Emma beamed, filled with self-respect. I appreciate you forcing me to step outside my comfort zone.

Jack beamed a broad grin. That's why we have partners, right?

Emma felt as though she were floating back to the car. She felt empowered by her newfound assurance after overcoming her fear. She was prepared to face any difficulties that might arise.

In addition, she realized that with Jack by her side, she could accomplish anything.

Chapter 8: Falling in Love All Over Again

Since moving in together almost a year ago, Emma and Jack's affection for one another has only deepened. Together, they had persevered through adversity and created a life they both enjoyed.

Jack planned a romantic supper at home for Emma one night and surprised her with it. The table was decorated with candles and flowers, and he had prepared her favorite dinner.

During their meal, Jack gave Emma a serious look. "Emma, I have to tell you something."

The nerves began to overtake Emma. What dire warning could he possibly be delivering?

Jack inhaled deeply. "I want to spend the rest of my life with you, Emma. I love you more than anything in the world."

Emma felt a sudden fluttering in her heart. Jack, are you...are you proposing to me?

With a modest grin on his face, Jack nodded. That's right; "Emma, will you marry me?"

Emma felt her eyes well up with tears. Never before in her life had she felt such joy. I will say, "Sure, Jack."

Emma and Jack were hugging one other so tightly that it was like falling in love all over again. She couldn't believe her good fortune in finding a man who cared about her so much that he wanted to spend the rest of his life with her.

They talked about their future plans for the rest of the night. A quiet wedding on the beach and a honeymoon in Europe were among the arrangements that Jack had already begun preparing.

Emma felt as though she were a character in a fantastical story. She was engaged to the man of her dreams when she had given up hope of ever finding love again.

Emma looked at Jack as they kissed passionately on the couch. We're getting married? I can't believe it.

Jack beamed a broad grin. I feel the same way, but I know that we will be happy together, Emma. Forever.

A wave of calmness washed through Emma. She had accepted Jack's truthfulness. Together, they had overcome many difficulties and made a life. They'd established mutual trust and an unconditional love for one another.

They were now destined to spend forever together, creating a life of joy, excitement, and love.

Emma felt like she was falling in love with Jack for the first time as they kissed. And she realized that their journey together was only beginning.

Chapter 9: A Promise to Keep

Emma was both excited and nervous as the wedding day drew near. She was never comfortable in front of a large group of people, and the prospect of a public performance made her nervous.

This, however, was exactly what she had in mind. She was ready to make a lifelong commitment to Jack by getting married.

Emma felt like she was in a dream as she walked down the aisle with her father at her side. She looked down the hall and saw Jack waiting for her, his eyes aglow with affection.

Emma was overcome with emotion as they said their vows. Her commitment to love and care for Jack for the rest of her life was a solemn one, and she intended to keep it.

Dancing, speeches, and an abundance of food and drink made the reception a whirlwind of activity. Emma felt like she was encased in a protective bubble of positivity and affection.

Nearing the end of the evening, Jack reached for Emma's hand. Can we get going now?

Emma nodded, a wave of fatigue overtaking her. She was desperate to get to bed and rest.

Jack gave her a stern look as they strolled to the car. "Emma, I have to tell you something."

Emma experienced a wave of anxiety. I don't know what he could possible say at this point.

Jack inhaled deeply. "Emma, I want you to know that no matter what, no matter where in the world life may lead us, I will always love you."

Emma felt her eyes well up with tears. "I agree with you, Jack; I adore you and will always be there for you."

Jack's eyes wrinkled up in a grin. That's all the confirmation I need.

Emma felt a wave of appreciation rush over her as they drove home. She finally found someone who could love her no matter what, someone who would pledge to be there for her no matter what.

She promised, and she knew she would keep it. She promised Jack that no matter what happened, she would be there for him.

Emma felt as like she were in a dream as they slid into bed, fatigued but content. It was a dream, though, from which she did not wish to awake. She had finally found her soul mate, and she intended to devote the rest of her life to keeping their love alive and well.

Chapter 10: The First Date

Although Emma and Jack had been roommates for nearly a year, they had never actually gone on a date. They had spent countless nights together in the kitchen or in front of the television, but they had never gone out on the town.

Jack planned a surprise dinner for Emma at an exclusive restaurant in the city one night. He rented a suit, and Emma shopped for hours to find the ideal dress.

Emma was overcome with anticipation as they walked into the restaurant. This was a first for her, and she was excited to see what the evening held.

Jack grinned at Emma as they took their seats at the table. The beauty in you really shines tonight.

Emma's face flushed with delight. You're rather handsome yourself, so thank you.

Emma's nerves began to kick in as they examined the menu. I mean, what if she accidentally dropped her food or her dress?

Jack, though, was there to lead the way, advise wisely, and put her at rest.

Emma was in a heavenly state when the food began to come. She had never had such luxurious and exotic flavors.

Emma sensed a bond developing with her new friend as they chatted and laughed together. There was a buzz and a sense of anticipation in the air, unlike their typical evenings in.

As they had cleaned their plates, Jack gave Emma a stern look. "Emma, I have to tell you something."

Emma experienced a wave of anxiety. Is there anything he could possibly say?

Jack inhaled deeply. Though we've been roommates for some time, I still want Emma to know how much she means to me and how much I can't picture my life without her.

Emma felt her eyes well up with tears. It meant the world to her because Jack had never said anything like that before.

Her voice cracked with passion as she answered, "I love you too, Jack." Above and above anything else.

Emma had the sensation of floating as they returned to the car after leaving the restaurant. For her, this was the most memorable night ever, and she looked forward to many more wonderful experiences with Jack in the years to come.

Back at their flat, Emma felt a wave of satisfaction as they cuddled on the couch. She had finally found her soul mate, and she intended to devote the rest of her life to keeping their love alive and well.

Chapter 11: A Surprising Turn of Events

After a few years of marriage, Emma and Jack enjoyed the ideal life together. Together, they created a beautiful haven of joy and laughter.

Nevertheless, Emma's sister called her up with some unexpected news one day. Tragically, their father had recently passed away.

Emma was overcome with feelings of disbelief and loss. Since she and Jack had left their hometown to start a new life together, she and her father had not been in contact.

But suddenly she was overcome with remorse. Before it was too late, she wished she had tried to make amends with him.

When she sobbed, Jack wrapped his arms around her and offered soothing words. We will get through this together, and I am here for you, Emma.

Emma was nervous as they drove to her father's burial. She was worried about how her mother would react to her return home.

But, Emma felt a sense of relief as she spotted her mother waiting for her at the airport, tears flowing down her face. The woman who raised her gave her a bear embrace and told her daughter how much she had missed her.

For the first time in years, Emma felt a closeness to her family when they all gathered for the funeral. Emma felt that she was getting to know her father for the first time through these reminiscences and conversations.

Emma's mom took her aside as they were getting ready to go. "Emma, there's something I have to tell you."

Emma experienced a wave of anxiety. Is there anything her mom could possibly say to her?

Emma, in the will your father left you a house in a tiny town not too far from here.

Emma's mouth dropped open in shock. A dwelling? Why would he leave a house to his daughter?

Emma was nervous as they drove into the small town. To what would they be exposed?

Emma felt as though she were in a dream as they pulled up to the house. It was an impressive Victorian estate with a wide front porch and a spacious backyard.

Emma felt like she was digging up buried treasure as they explored the mansion. There was so much old stuff there that it made her feel like she'd gone back in time.

As they turned in for the night, Emma felt a calm come over her. Her dad gave her this house so she could start over.

They were starting a new chapter in their life as she snuggled up to Jack. And she was looking forward to going wherever it led.

Chapter 12: A Heartfelt Confession

For the past few months, Emma and Jack have been living in the house left to her by her father, and they couldn't be happier. The village was tranquil and charming, and they had even made a few new acquaintances there.

But as they watched the sunset from the porch one night, Jack turned to Emma and seemed quite serious.

"Emma, I have to tell you something."

Emma experienced a wave of anxiety. Is there anything he could possibly say?

Jack inhaled deeply. "I hope Emma understands how much she means to me. I'd rather die than have to live without you, and my love for you knows no bounds."

Emma felt her eyes well up with tears. Jack had told her he loved her numerous times before, but this time it was different.

As Jack spoke, Emma's heart seemed to expand to hold all the love in the world. This was the husband she had chosen, the one she would spend the rest of her life with. And his affection for her was unmatched.

As Jack was done, Emma rushed over and gave him a bear hug. "Likewise, Jack, I adore you. As much as possible."

Emma felt unstoppable as they sat there, hugging each other. She had discovered her soul mate, and he adored her without conditions.

Even when the sky turned pink and orange as the sun sank behind them, Emma knew that their adventure together was only beginning.

Chapter 13: A Complicated Family Dynamic

Shortly after arriving in their new hometown with Jack, Emma got a call from her sister. Her mother's illness required her attention.

Emma experienced a wave of anxiety. Their relationship had always been tense, but since her father's death, she hadn't seen her mother.

Yet, she was aware that she had to leave. Jack stood by her side, providing moral support.

Fear began to creep into Emma as they approached her mother's home. After so much time had passed, she wondered how her mother would react to finally meeting her again.

As they hugged each other, however, Emma felt a wave of comfort wash over her. Her mother may have appeared weak and feeble, but she was still the same strong person within.

Emma felt like she was getting to know her mother better than ever as they established a pattern for taking care of her. Emma felt like they were making up after their conversation and shared laughter.

Nevertheless, as the weeks progressed, Emma's mother deteriorated. Emma and Jack stayed up with her through the night when she was hospitalized.

During their conversation, Emma's mom revealed secrets she had never shared with her before. She opened up to Emma about the hardships she had endured and the choices she now deeply regretted.

When empathy washed over Emma, she felt compelled to help. Like her, her mother had trouble making head or tail of a confusing environment.

Emma's mom reached over and grabbed her hand as they sat down. "Emma, there's something I need to tell you. I apologize for everything I've done and wish I could change the past."

Emma felt her eyes well up with tears. Never before had she heard her mother express such contrition.

As her mother went on, Emma felt a tremendous relief wash over her. They were still a family despite their strange dynamic. One another's love united them.

When they left the hospital that night, Emma felt like she was looking at the world through other eyes. She had reconciled with her mother, and she felt optimistic about the future of their relationship.

And when she clung to Jack's hand, she felt the unconditional love and support that would carry her through any difficulties.

Chapter 14: A Romantic Getaway

Emma and Jack had been working hard and meeting new acquaintances in their new city. But, they agreed that they needed a break to regroup and spend some quality time together.

So the two of them made plans to embark on a romantic trip together. They came across a rustic cabin beside a peaceful lake and decided to stay there.

Emma felt a wave of calm rush over her as they approached the cottage. This was a godsend for them.

After unpacking and settling into the cabin, Emma and Jack spent their days hiking and canoeing on the lake and in the surrounding forests.

They spent their evenings drinking wine together in front of the fire while discussing their aspirations for the future.

One night while they watched the stars from the porch, Jack turned to Emma with a solemn expression on his face.

I need to tell you something, Emma.

Emma experienced a wave of anxiety. Is there anything he could possibly say?

Jack inhaled deeply. "I want you to know, Emma, that despite all we've been through together, I'm ready to spend the rest of my life with you. I hope to spend the rest of my life with you, laughing and exploring the world together."

Emma felt her eyes well up with tears. This was the husband she had chosen, the one she would spend the rest of her life with. And his affection for her was unmatched.

Emma felt as though she were in a dream as she gave him a bear embrace. This man was her soul mate, and he promised to be with her for the rest of time.

As they continued their vacation together, Emma couldn't help but feel like she was falling in love with him all over again. They had created a life together, but now they could revisit their roots and recall the spark that had ignited their partnership.

Emma understood that her love and adventures with Jack were only beginning when they left the cottage and returned to their lives in the tiny town.

Chapter 15: A Bump in the Road

Emma and Jack had been steadily constructing a life together full of love and joy in their sleepy little town. Nevertheless, one day Emma got some disturbing news from her doctor.

She needed a biopsy after discovering a lump in her breast.

A wave of terror washed over Emma. The prospect of cancer was horrifying, especially because she had never experienced anything like this before.

Jack was there, supporting her and bringing comfort by holding her hand. "Emma, I know that we can get through this. In other words, you can count on me."

Emma felt like she was in a daze while they waited for the biopsy results. She was unable to think about or concentrate on anything else.

Yet the good news is that the outcomes were confirmed by the tests. Emma was diagnosed with breast cancer.

Emma and Jack sat together and embraced one other firmly while they sobbed. This was an obstacle that would require their combined effort to overcome.

Jack remained by Emma's side through it all when she began her treatments. Throughout her chemotherapy treatments, he held her hand, fed her well, and bolstered her optimism.

Emma was overcome by feelings of appreciation. She finally discovered her soul mate, the man who would always be there for her.

Emma's therapy worked over the course of several months, and she eventually went into remission. Every day, every second spent with Jack, she counted as a blessing.

When they watched the sunset together on the porch, Emma felt like they had been through a war. Yet now they were more resilient and in love than ever before.

This was her husband, the one who had stood by her side through every difficulty. Together, with love and resolve, she was confident they could overcome any obstacle.

Chapter 16: Uncovering the Truth

Emma and Jack had been married for a few years and had settled down in the tiny town. Nevertheless, Emma's life was forever altered when a letter arrived in the mail.

A lawyer had written to tell her that her father's will was being challenged. Her father had left the house to her, but someone was now claiming it as their own.

Both fury and perplexity washed over Emma. The one thing her father had left her seemed to be under attack.

As Emma and Jack dug deeper into the case, they learned that the individual challenging the will was a distant cousin. She said Emma's dad promised it to her even though she'd never met him.

Emma felt as though she were unraveling a complex web of dishonesty and lies. What kind of greedy person would try to grab what wasn't theirs?

Emma felt a surge of resolve as they readied themselves for trial. She would defend the inheritance her father had given her at any cost.

And as they walked inside the courtroom, Emma's nerves began to take hold. But she was resolved to hold her ground and fight for what was rightfully hers.

Emma and Jack argued their case with poise and conviction as the trial progressed. They proved that Emma's father had left her money and other gifts in his will.

And the judge sided with them in the end. Emma's distant cousin was made to pay her legal bills after she was awarded the house.

Emma felt a huge burden being lifted off her shoulders as they left the courthouse. Truth had been revealed, and she felt that justice had been done.

And on the way back to their little town house, Emma felt like a new chapter was beginning in her life. She had met adversity head-on and emerged from it more resilient and resolute than before.

Chapter 17: A Moment of Doubt

Emma and Jack had been constructing a contented life in their hometown, but one day, Emma was overcome by doubt about their relationship.

Is this the life she really desired? Was she making the right decisions by tying the knot with Jack and moving to a small town?

Emma felt like she was in a haze as the persistent uncertainty weighed on her. She was unable to divert her attention elsewhere or take pleasure in the things that had previously brought her pleasure.

Jack observed her transformation and expressed worry. "Emma, are you all right? What's going on?"

In the end, Emma was unable to tell him the truth. She worried that he would be hurt or disapprove of her because of it.

Emma felt further and further away from Jack as the weeks turned into months. They had established a life together, but she still doubted whether or not it was the one she desired.

However, as they sat on the porch one day, Jack looked at her seriously. I want you to know that I love you more than anything in the world, and I can't picture my life without you, but I also want you to know that I want you to be happy, really happy, so please tell me anything you need to.

A huge burden had been removed from Emma's shoulders. No matter what she did, Jack loved her. And she knew that she needed to be honest with him.

Jack, I've been having doubts about our life together lately. I'm not sure if this is what I want or if I should be looking elsewhere.

Jack looked at her with a compassionate expression. "Emma, I understand. And I want you to know that I support you, no matter what. If there's something else you need to explore, then let's explore it together."

Tears began to well up in Emma's eyes. She had married this man because he loved her without condition.

As they discussed their emotions, Emma began to feel a sense of clarity. Perhaps she didn't belong in this small town, but the world still held possibilities.

And she had complete faith that Jack would be there for her, cheering her on no matter what.

Chapter 18: Holding On to Hope

Both Emma and Jack had been through a lot, but when they got some news, it really tested them.

Sarah, Jack's sister, was suffering from a rare and deadly form of cancer. Sarah was given a grim prognosis, with only a few months to live.

Emma's heart seemed to be breaking as they visited Sarah in the hospital. Sarah was still in the prime of her life in her early 30s.

But Sarah was a tough competitor. She persisted in her optimism despite mounting obstacles.

The more time Emma and Jack spent with Sarah, the more they admired her bravery and strength. She was never one to whine or give up.

Sarah's condition, however, deteriorated as the weeks turned into months. She had frequent hospitalizations, and the treatments appeared to be having an adverse effect on her health.

Both Emma and Jack felt like their emotions were being thrown all over the place. Sarah would appear to be improving, only to end up in the hospital again the next day.

Nonetheless, they continued to have faith. They refused to give up hope that Sarah would survive, that a miracle was still possible.

Emma and Jack devoted their time to Sarah as much as they could as her health deteriorated. They reminisced, told stories, and laughed until they cried.

Sarah turned to them with a wan smile as they sat by her bedside one day.

She gushed, "I love you both so much." "I appreciate your hope and your presence here today."

Tears welled up in Emma and Jack's eyes. Sarah was the most resilient person they knew, and she showed them the value of faith and affection.

Some days later, when Sarah passed away, Emma and Jack felt as if they had been through a war. But in the end, they knew that they had not given up hope.

Emma knew she would never forget Sarah's bravery as they left the hospital holding each other close. She had been motivational, a symbol of the strength of faith in the face of adversity.

Chapter 19: A Life-Changing Decision

Emma and Jack had settled into a comfortable routine in their small town, but that all changed when Emma received an unexpected offer.

A job offer from a big city law firm meant she would have to leave the small town and the life she'd built with Jack.

Both excitement and nervousness washed over Emma. This was a once-in-a-lifetime chance for her to take her career to new heights.

The problem is that she would have to abandon the life she had created with Jack. Their family and friends, their shared life.

Emma could tell that Jack was conflicted as they discussed the offer. He hoped she would be happy, but he wasn't sure he was ready to leave their hometown.

As they worked through their emotions together, Emma began to realize the magnitude of the choice she was about to make. She could advance her career by taking this opportunity, but it would require her to leave the home she had made with Jack.

Emma realized that she had to go with her gut in the end. She could now venture forth and test her mettle in ways she had never before considered possible.

She felt her excitement and anticipation growing as she accepted the job offer. This was a fresh start for her, an opportunity to discover uncharted territories.

However, it was also an opportunity to finalize the relationship she had built with Jack. Emma felt as though she were leaving a piece of herself behind as they packed up their house and said goodbye to their friends.

But she knew that she had to seize this opportunity in order to broaden her horizons and pursue her passions. As they left the town, Emma knew she would never forget the home she and Jack had created together. She looked back on that time in her life with fondness; she had accomplished a lot and felt fulfilled.

However, the current situation called for a new beginning. A brand new beginning full of exciting prospects and interesting challenges.

Chapter 20: A Love Tested

After several years of marriage, Emma and Jack had created a wonderful life together. But one day they were confronted with a difficulty that would put their love through tests it had never before experienced.

Jack was offered a job on the other side of the country, but it would require him to travel extensively and be gone for extended periods of time.

Emma was overcome by feelings of dread and anxiety. How would they manage such a long separation? Would their love be able to last if they were to be separated for so long?

Over the course of their conversation, Emma and Jack realized that this was a great opportunity for him to expand his horizons professionally.

But it also meant spending time apart, which was something neither of them had ever done before.

After Jack had left for his new job, Emma felt empty. Never before had she felt so hopeless and abandoned.

However, they committed to maintaining regular communication via phone and video chat. Whenever they were together, they would treasure every moment.

Emma and Jack met the challenge head-on and grew closer to each other as the months passed. They shared their dreams and hopes with each other over the phone every day.

They made the most of their time together during the times that Jack was able to return home for visits. They went out of their way to experience new things and one another.

It wasn't simple, though. The separation was difficult, the time apart trying. They knew they would make it through this because of the love they had for each other.

They felt like they had been through a war together as Jack finished his job and returned home to Emma. However, they had emerged from the ordeal even stronger and more in love than before.

This was a tried and true love that had stood the test of time and separation. It was a love that had overcome hardships and come out on top, a love that had triumphed.

As they clung to each other, Emma and Jack knew their love would endure no matter how long it had been apart. They had persevered through adversity as a couple and emerged even closer and more devoted to one another.

Chapter 21: The Power of Forgiveness

After several years of marriage, Emma and Jack had created a wonderful life together. But then they had to deal with a problem that could have broken them up forever.

Emma had made a terrible error, and it had caused Jack a lot of pain. The trust she had earned from him had been betrayed, and he felt no hope of ever forgiving her.

Emma felt regret wash over her as they discussed their emotions. The man she loved more than anything in the world had been hurt by her mistake.

But Jack felt betrayed, angry, and uncertain about whether or not he could ever forgive her.

Emma began to fear that she was losing the man she loved as the days turned into weeks. She realized she was in the wrong but had no idea how to put things right.

But then she heard a story that altered her life forever. She had been inspired to forgive and move on by the story of another woman who had been in a similar situation.

A switch in Emma's brain turned on, and she suddenly realized something. Perhaps there was still a chance to make amends, to show Jack how much she cared about him and how sorry she was for what had happened.

She could see Jack's heart opening as she told him the woman's story. Perhaps there was a way to forget the past and embrace the future.

As a result, Emma and Jack took their first steps toward reconciliation. They had a heart-to-heart, told each other what they hoped for the future, and set about mending their broken trust in one another.

Their love wasn't easy to maintain, but it was worth the effort. They were both relieved and lighter as they finally managed to forgive each other.

Together, they had overcome adversity, emerging stronger and more dedicated than before.

Therein lay the strength of forgiveness, the ability to forget hurtful things and look forward with kindness and understanding.

They knew their love for each other was stronger than any mistake or betrayal as Emma and Jack held each other close. They were able to let the past go and move forward in love and understanding.

Chapter 22: Building a Future Together

Despite the hardships they had endured, Emma and Jack had managed to create a fulfilling life together. And eventually they made the commitment to continue their journey together.

They had considered starting a family for some time, but ultimately decided that the time was now.

Feelings of both excitement and nervousness washed over Emma as they began their journey to parenthood. She knew that this new phase of their lives together would bring both new challenges and new opportunities.

Emma and Jack were expecting their first child and were working together to secure a bright future for their growing family. As they looked ahead to the years ahead, they shared their aspirations and plans.

And as their family grew, so did the difficulties they had to overcome. But they overcame the odds by sticking together and fighting like mad.

Together, they created a life that was rich with affection, hilarity, and happiness. Emma and Jack knew they had made the right choice when they saw their children flourish under their care.

Their future together was just beginning, and it was full of promise. They knew that whatever the future held, they would do it together, with love and strength, and they were excited about the years ahead.

Chapter 23: A Celebration of Love

After several years of marriage, Emma and Jack had created a wonderful life together. And one day, in honor of their love, they decided to renew their vows.

Emma and Jack were overcome with happiness and anticipation as they planned the party. This was a chance to publicly declare their love for one another and renew their vows to one another.

Emma and Jack's excitement grew as the party's big day drew near. Everything was meticulously planned because they wanted this to be a party they would always remember.

And as they stood there before their loved ones, they were filled with joy and love. They renewed their vows of love and dedication to one another.

The love and happiness that surrounded Emma and Jack during the celebration was palpable. They celebrated with dancing, humor, and reminiscing.

It was a joyous occasion to commemorate the love they shared and to renew their vows to one another.

And by the time the festivities ended, Emma and Jack believed they were the luckiest people alive. They had finally found each other, were settling into married life, and were confident in the strength of their love.

It was a chance to celebrate their love and remind their friends and family of the strength of their bond. Emma and Jack left the party hand in hand, confident that their love and happiness would last for many years to come.

Chapter 24: The Wedding Day

Emma and Jack had been together for several years, and they had built a happy life together. And one day, they decided to take the next step in their journey together - to get married.

As they planned their wedding day, Emma and Jack felt a sense of joy and excitement wash over them. This was the day they had been waiting for, a chance to exchange vows and pledge their love and commitment to each other in front of their loved ones.

As the day of the wedding approached, Emma felt a sense of nervousness wash over her. This was the biggest day of her life, and she wanted everything to be perfect.

But as she walked down the aisle, towards Jack, she felt like she was in a dream. She looked around at their loved ones, all gathered together to celebrate their love, and felt like she was the luckiest woman in the world.

As they exchanged vows and rings, Emma and Jack felt like they were the only two people in the world. They promised to love and cherish each other, to be there for each other through thick and thin.

And as they shared their first dance as husband and wife, Emma felt like her heart was bursting with love and happiness.

This was the wedding day, the day that they would remember for the rest of their lives. And as they celebrated with their loved ones, Emma and Jack knew that they had made the right decision in choosing each other.

They had found true love, a love that would last a lifetime. And as they looked ahead to the years to come, they knew that they would face whatever challenges came their way, together, in love and commitment.

Chapter 25: Happily Ever After

Emma and Jack had been together for a long time and had overcome many obstacles together. Nonetheless, despite everything, they managed to build a life together that was full of love, laughter, and happiness.

When Emma and Jack reflected on their journey together, they were overcome with feelings of appreciation and joy. They had discovered the love of a lifetime in each other.

Together, in love and commitment, they faced the future years confident that they could overcome any obstacles that might arise.

Their love and happiness brought them a happily ever after. Together, they had created a life to be proud of: a home, a family, and a career.

They looked at each other, hand in hand, and realized they had made the right choice. They had discovered true love, a love that would last no matter what came their way.

And as Emma and Jack celebrated their love, they realized they were the luckiest people alive. They had finally connected and established a loving and joyful life together.

Their happily ever after was a life of love, laughter, and happiness. They were looking forward to the years ahead, confident that they would be able to overcome any obstacles that came their way because of their undying love and devotion to one another.

It was a story of second chances and eternal love, and it was theirs to tell forever.

Chapter 26: Memories to Last a Lifetime

Emma and Jack realized as they reflected on their life together that they had created indelible memories.

They had explored the world, done exciting things, and created a life together that was bursting at the seams with happiness.

They had been tested and tried, but they had persevered and supported one another through it all.

They realized their love story was one they would always remember as they reflected on their time together.

They had created a life together that was rich in happy recollections, from their wedding day to the births of their children.

They'd spent countless hours together, sharing everything from laughter to silence. And as they reflected on their years together, they realized that their love was solid enough to weather any storm.

They knew they had found a love that would last a lifetime because it was a story of redemption and true love.

And Emma and Jack, looking ahead to the years to come, knew that they would continue to create memories that would last a lifetime.

They would always be there for each other emotionally and physically, and they would treasure the time they spent together.

Theirs was a story of finding each other and creating a life together full of love and laughter and joy.

As they hugged, Emma and Jack knew their love would endure no matter what came their way. They had created a life together full of memories that would last forever, and they were confident that new chapters in their love story would be written for many years to come.

Also by Harper Knight

The Last Dance: A Love Affair with Destiny
A Love to Remember: A Tale of Redemption and True Love

About the Publisher

Accepting manuscripts in the most categories. We love to help people get their words available to the world.

Revival Waves of Glory focus is to provide more options to be published. We do traditional paperbacks, hardcovers, audio books and ebooks all over the world. A traditional royalty-based publisher that offers self-publishing options, Revival Waves provides a very author friendly and transparent publishing process, with President Bill Vincent involved in the full process of your book. Send us your manuscript and we will contact you as soon as possible.

Contact: Bill Vincent at rwgpublishing@yahoo.com

www.ingramcontent.com/pod-product-compliance
Lightning Source LLC
LaVergne TN
LVHW042000060526
838200LV00041B/1808